With all my love to Nancy, my darling wife,
I dreamed of you for all my life.
And for our children Brennan, Avery, Sabrina and Ryan,
you're all beautiful, dreams come true and I'm not lyin'.

- JTG

Rainstorm

This edition published by Parragon Books Ltd in 2018 and distributed by:
Parragon Inc. • 440 Park Avenue South, 13th Floor • New York, NY 10016, U.S.A. • Copyright © Parragon Books Ltd 2018
Written by Joseph T. Garcia • Illustrated by Kimberley Barnes • Edited by Sarah Bradshaw • Designed by Lizzy Doyle • Production by Michaela Bartzsch • Prepress by Michael Penman

Dream You'll Be

Rainstorm

Go to bed each sleepy child,
and dream what dreams you might.

Dreaming's good most anytime,
but especially at night.

Dream you'll be a **movie star**
with your name lit up in lights,

or that you'll be a **superhero**
flying around in tights.

Would you like to be a **doctor** saving people's lives?

Or perhaps a **beekeeper**, tending buzzing hives?

What if you're a **musketeer**
fighting battles with your sword?

Or a world-class **surfer**

catching waves upon your board?

Maybe you're an **architect**
designing a brand new city.

Or are you a **writer** telling stories warm and witty?

You could be a
brave **firefighter**
running through a fire,

or a fearless **acrobat**
high upon a wire.

Perchance you'll
be a **dancer** leaping
across the floor,

or maybe a **soccer star**
with the winning score.

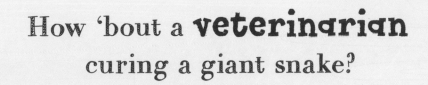

How 'bout a **veterinarian**
curing a giant snake?

VeT

Or a skillful **baker** baking a giant cake?

See yourself as a **teacher**
helping children think,

or a figure **skater**
gliding around a rink.

You'd make a fine **police officer** saving people in distress, or a bold **explorer** finding the monster of Loch Ness.

LOCH NESS XPRESS

Imagine you're an **astronaut**
bouncing on the moon,

or maybe you're a famous **rocker** belting out a tune.

Dream that you're a **pirate** sailing oceans blue,

or a brilliant **scientist**
finding something new.

Do you wish you were a **pilot** soaring to great heights?

Or a clever **artist** painting
the world's great sights?

Maybe you're a **mountaineer** climbing to the summit,

or a fearless **skydiver** whose job it is to plummet.

You could be a
football player winning
games with teammates,

or maybe you're the
President of these **United States!**

This world is full of many things
to dream that you can be. Just remember you're already
the most precious thing to me.

Now close your eyes each sleepy child and dream
what dreams you may. I'll see you in
the morning when you start a brand new day.

FLYING